ELMO'S BEST THANKSGIVING EVER!

By Jodie Shepherd
Illustrated by Shane Clester

A GOLDEN BOOK · NEW YORK

© 2022 Sesame Workshop®, Sesame Street®, and associated characters, trademarks, and design elements are owned and licensed by Sesame Workshop. All rights reserved. Published in the United States by Golden Books, an imprint of Random House Children's Books, a division of Penguin Random House LLC, 1745 Broadway, New York, NY 10019, and in Canada by Penguin Random House Canada Limited, Toronto, in conjunction with Sesame Workshop. Golden Books, A Golden Book, A Little Golden Book, the G colophon, and the distinctive gold spine are registered trademarks of Penguin Random House LLC.
rhcbooks.com
www.sesamestreet.org
Educators and librarians, for a variety of teaching tools, visit us at
RHTeachersLibrarians.com
ISBN 978-0-593-48311-4 (trade) — ISBN 978-0-593-48312-1 (ebook)
Printed in the United States of America
10 9 8 7 6 5 4 3 2 1

Elmo woke up on the morning of Thanksgiving.
It was pouring outside.

"Oh no!" the little red monster cried.
"How will Elmo's friends have an outdoor
Thanksgiving dinner if it's raining?"

Elmo's mommy tried to cheer him up. "We can move the celebration indoors, Elmo," she said. "The important thing is to share the holiday with the people and monsters you love."

Elmo's daddy said, "Why don't you ask your friends what they are thankful for? And don't forget your umbrella."

Elmo went outside. The rain was still coming down. Elmo's umbrella kept him dry. Oscar was soaking wet, though.

"Would you like to share Elmo's umbrella, Oscar?" Elmo asked the grouch.

"Grouches don't like sharing,"
Oscar reminded Elmo. "Besides,
I *love* the rain. It makes me soaking
wet. I'm thankful for *that*!"

Elmo saw Abby coming down the street.
"Hi, Abby," Elmo greeted her. "Elmo just
learned that Oscar actually *likes* the rain.
Do you?"

"Yes, I'm thankful for the rain, too," Abby answered. "The flowers in my garden need it to grow."

"Hi, Bert! Hi, Ernie!" Elmo called out to his friends. "Elmo wonders if you are thankful for rain."

"Well, we're thankful for rain *puddles*," Ernie told him. "They're one of Rubber Duckie's favorite things."

"Pigeons like splashing in puddles, too,"
added Bert.

"Elmo guesses rain isn't so bad," Elmo said to
himself as he continued down Sesame Street.

Cookie Monster was busy baking pies
for the party later that day. So many pies!
"Cookie Monster! What is going on
here?" Elmo asked.

"Some pies too lumpy. Some pies too crumbly," Cookie Monster explained. "So me eat the mistakes. Me thankful for dee-licious mistakes!"

Elmo giggled.

"Me always say, 'If at first me don't succeed, then try pie again.' So do not worry. Me will have perfect pie at Thanksgiving meal."

"Wow! Cookie Monster is thankful for making mistakes," Elmo said, going on his way. "Elmo didn't realize there were so many things to be thankful for."

He spied some friends in the
Community Center, and he went inside.

Julia was busy painting a picture of her friends Rosita and Big Bird, who were making music together. Julia looked up and saw Elmo. "Pretty music," she said.

"Music makes everyone feel good," agreed Big Bird.

"So Elmo guesses you're all thankful for music," said the little red monster. "And painting," he added.

Elmo hummed along a little bit, then waved
to his friends. "See you later at Thanksgiving
dinner!" he called as he left for home.

That afternoon, there was a wonderful
feast at Elmo's house. Everybody was there!

It was the best Thanksgiving celebration ever! Elmo was so lucky to be part of it. He realized that it didn't matter what the weather was like. Being with the people he loved—and the people who loved him—made the day perfect.

Elmo was thankful for his family, for good food, and for good friends. He was even thankful for . . . the rain!

"Elmo loves rain," Elmo decided when he and two of his friends went outside after dessert. "Especially when there's a big umbrella to share!"